THE ROGUE BODYGUARD

A 19TH CENTURY ERA EROTIC SHORT STORY

ELIZA FINCH

1

——————

"Elizabeth!" yelled Mr. Montague as his 21 year old beautiful daughter pushed her way towards the front door of the Montague Manor.

"You need to stay home tonight. It's not safe for you out there."

"Father, what on earth are you rambling about now?"

"Elizabeth, I am afraid I have angered a few people with my last business deal. You need to stay close to home for the time being."

"Nonsense. I am due to show myself at the Wellington ball this evening. I will be fine."

"Elizabeth! Listen to me. I have hired a guard to keep his eye on you until this threat passes. He is due to arrive here at any moment."

"A guard? Father, this is absurd. I am fine. Now please get out of my way so that I can go to the ball."

And with that, Elizabeth left.

Elizabeth's elderly father, Mr. Montague, was no match for his willful and defiant daughter. Since her mother died a few years ago, Elizabeth has been uncontrollable. Her father would like nothing more than for her to get married and settle down, but she was only interested in parties and escapades with men that set the tongues of the ton on fire with rumors and gossip. But, Elizabeth did not care, and Mr. Montague had mostly given up on trying to stop her.

His one last attempt was to hire a guard to watch over her. Maybe the guard will at least keep her in line and get her behavior under control.

As the clock struck seven, signaling the arrival of the appointed guard, Mr. Montague's anxiety grew. He paced back and forth in the opulent drawing room of Montague Manor, his heart pounding with each passing second. Would this guard be able to handle Elizabeth's spirited nature? Or would she simply charm him into submission like all the others?

The sound of footsteps echoing through the grand hallway interrupted Mr. Montague's thoughts. He hurriedly straightened his waistcoat and adjusted his cravat before making his way to the door.

A tall, brooding figure emerged from the shadows, clad in a black suit that seemed to blend seamlessly with the night itself. His dark eyes held an intensity that hinted at a troubled past, and Mr. Montague felt a twinge of unease.

"Are you the man assigned to protect my daughter?" Mr. Montague asked tentatively.

The guard nodded curtly, his voice deep and commanding. "Yes, I am. My name is James Blackwood, and I assure you, Mr. Montague, your daughter will be safe under my watch."

Mr. Montague let out a sigh of relief, though a small part of him still doubted whether anyone could truly control Elizabeth's rebellious spirit. He led James into the drawing room, where the walls were adorned with portraits of their ancestors, all watching with stern gazes.

As they walked, Mr. Montague thought about how Elizabeth

had inherited her mother's beauty—her dark curls and captivating eyes were enough to ensnare any man's heart. But beneath that enchanting facade lay a restless soul that craved excitement and freedom.

"Miss Elizabeth has already left for the ball," Mr. Montague explained. "She was not happy about the idea of having a guard. You will need to go find her. She may resist your presence at first, but I implore you to remain steadfast in your duty."

James' lips curved into a wry smile. "I've dealt with strong-willed women before, Mr. Montague, and I can assure you, I won't be swayed easily."

With a nod of determination, James turned on his heel and made his way towards the door, leaving Mr. Montague to worry in the safety of Montague Manor. The night air was cool and crisp as he stepped out into the sprawling gardens surrounding the estate, scanning the darkness for any sign of Elizabeth.

The moon bathed the grounds in an ethereal glow, casting long shadows that danced across the neatly trimmed hedges and intricate topiaries. James's senses were heightened as he ventured further away from the manor, his training kicking in.

As he navigated through the streets of London towards the Wellington ball, James wondered what kind of woman Elizabeth truly was. Mr. Montague painted a picture of an uncontrollable firecracker, but there was always more to someone beneath the surface. He hoped to discover a different side of her during their time together.

Finally arriving at the prestigious Wellington ball, James was met with a sea of elegantly dressed couples twirling and mingling in the grand ballroom. He allowed his eyes to scan the room, searching for a woman who matched Mr. Montague's description of Elizabeth.

There, across the room, he spotted her. Elizabeth Montague stood out effortlessly amongst the crowd. Her gown clung to her curves, accentuating her figure in all the right places. Her laughter rang through the air as she flirted with a gentleman at her side, her eyes sparkling mischievously.

James approached cautiously, weaving through the mass of dancing bodies. His presence went unnoticed by Elizabeth at first, as she was engrossed in her conversation. He stood back and watched and listened.

In the dimly lit ballroom, Elizabeth moved gracefully through the throng of suitors, her raven hair cascading down her back. Her eyes sparkled with mischief, and her full lips curled into a knowing smile as she navigated the sea of men who were vying for her attention, not noticing James yet. As the only daughter of a wealthy businessman, Elizabeth was a fiercely intelligent and determined young heiress. Though unmarried, she was flirtatious and notorious for her dalliances, garnering a reputation that both intrigued and intimidated the high society.

"Ah, Miss Elizabeth, a pleasure to see you," crooned an older gentleman as he leaned in closer, his hot breath caressing her neck. Elizabeth feigned interest, her mind preoccupied with thoughts of maintaining the freedom and independence that she had grown to cherish.

"Indeed, Lord Wellington," Elizabeth replied coyly, batting her eyelashes at the man before her. "Tell me, have you heard any news about my father's latest business venture?"

"Ah yes, your father is quite the shrewd businessman," Lord Wellington said, his eyes lingering on her ample décolletage. "I hear the risks are great, but the potential rewards even greater."

Elizabeth pursed her lips, acutely aware of the dangers posed by her family's wealth and her elderly father's risky business deals. She knew all too well that the world of commerce was fraught with peril, and she would not allow herself to become a pawn in her father's game.

"Father thinks I should settle down and get married," she

mused aloud, swirling the wine in her glass. "But I refuse to be tied down like some helpless damsel." Her voice was laced with determination, and she glanced sidelong at Lord Wellington, daring him to challenge her stance.

"Such a shame," Lord Wellington sighed, his fingers brushing the back of her hand. "A woman like you, Miss Elizabeth, deserves a man who can appreciate your... finer qualities."

"Indeed," she agreed, withdrawing her hand from his grasp. "But it seems such a man is hard to find in this den of wolves."

"Perhaps," Lord Wellington conceded, a wicked grin spreading across his face. "But I assure you, my dear, the hunt can be quite... exhilarating."

Elizabeth felt a shiver run down her spine, a mix of excitement and apprehension. She knew that her refusal to marry would only embolden her admirers, but she was determined to maintain her independence at all costs, even if it meant defying her father's wishes.

"Thank you for the advice, Lord Wellington," she replied coolly, disentangling herself from his lecherous gaze. "Now, if you'll excuse me, I have other matters to attend to." And with that, she turned on her heel and disappeared into the crowd, leaving the old lord to ponder the enigma that was Elizabeth.

Elizabeth stepped out onto the balcony, seeking a moment of respite from the stifling atmosphere of the ballroom. The cool night air caressed her exposed skin, making her shiver with anticipation. She leaned on the railing, her mind wandering to the recent conversation with Lord Wellington.

"Miss Elizabeth?" A deep, gravelly voice interrupted her thoughts.

She turned to find a tall, broad-shouldered man standing in the shadows, his features partly concealed by the darkness. Moonlight glinted off his chiseled jawline, revealing a strong, rugged face that sent a jolt of desire through her.

"Who are you?" she demanded, trying to suppress her sudden attraction.

"James," he replied simply. "Your father hired me as your personal guard. I am to fetch you home."

"Oh right. He mentioned something about that earlier today." Elizabeth scoffed. "I don't need a guard."

"Your father believes otherwise," James said, stepping closer. His muscled form was now fully visible, and Elizabeth admired the way his tailored suit clung to his powerful frame.

"Fine," she snapped, irritated at how easily her resolve had crumbled under his smoldering gaze. "But stay out of my way."

"Of course," James murmured, his eyes never leaving hers. The intensity of his stare made her feel both vulnerable and exhilarated.

"Can I trust you, James?" Elizabeth asked, her voice low and sultry.

"Absolutely, Miss Elizabeth," he replied, his voice rough with barely restrained passion. "I am here to protect you from any danger."

"Is that so?" she purred, stepping closer to him. The heat radiating from his body felt intoxicating, igniting a fire within her. "And what if the danger is you?"

"Then I'll take care of that too," he answered huskily, his gaze traveling over her curves with undisguised lust.

"Bold words," Elizabeth breathed, their faces mere inches apart. "Can you back them up?"

"Try me," he challenged, his voice thick with desire.

"Maybe I will," she whispered, her eyes locked on his full lips. She could practically taste the passion that already hung between them, a heady sensation that left her craving more.

"Miss Elizabeth..." James warned, his grip on her waist tightening as if to hold himself back from giving in to temptation.

"Call me Lizzie," she murmured, daring him to cross the line they both knew was dangerous but irresistible.

"Very well... Lizzie," he growled, and the sound sent shivers of anticipation coursing through her veins. She knew this was madness, but the thrill of defying her father's expectations by succumbing to her desires for the rugged guard was too enticing to resist.

"James," she whispered, her breath hot against his ear. "Show me how you plan to protect me."

"Your father was right. You are a tempting little wench. But I am not here to play games. It's time to go home."

Elizabeth was mortified. How dare he reject her advances like that.

"I am not leaving," she declared.

"You are. You can leave on your own volition, or I can carry you out of here in front of the Ton. Your choice."

Elizabeth glared at James, her emerald eyes burning with a mixture of anger and frustration. How dare he think he could control her, dictate her every move. She was not some fragile flower to be plucked and placed in a gilded cage. No, she was a force to be reckoned with; she was Elizabeth, the wild spirit that refused to be tamed.

With a defiant tilt of her chin, Elizabeth took a step forward, closing the distance between her and James until they were almost nose to nose. The tension crackled in the air as sparks of desire danced between them.

"You think you can just order me around?" she hissed, her voice edged with a dangerous intensity. "I am not one of your lackeys, James. I am Elizabeth Montague, and I will not be silenced or controlled."

James' eyes flashed with a mix of surprise and admiration, as if her fiery determination ignited a fire within him too. His grip on her waist loosened slightly, allowing for a fraction of space between their bodies.

"You're right," he admitted, his voice low and gravelly. "But understand this, Elizabeth - I am not here to control you. I am here to protect you. There are dangers lurking in the shadows."

Elizabeth's anger flickered, replaced by a flicker of curiosity. She had always been a woman of action, unafraid to face the unknown head-on. Perhaps this situation was no different.

"What kind of dangers?" she asked, her voice softer now, laced with a newfound vulnerability.

James hesitated for a moment, his eyes studying her face as if searching for the right words. "Your father's business dealings have attracted unwanted attention," he finally revealed. "There are whispers of rival factions and clandestine operations that seek to exploit your family's fortune. If you stay here tonight without proper protection, you'll be putting yourself in grave danger."

After a moment, Elizabeth's resolve softened.

"Very well. We can leave."

2

_____

The flickering glow of the dimly lit candles cast soft shadows across the opulent ballroom, as James and Elizabeth made their way discreetly towards the grand exit. The music played a haunting melody, which seemed to echo their own racing heartbeats.

"Quickly," Elizabeth whispered, her breath hot against James's ear. "No one must see us leave."

James nodded, his eyes darting around the room, ensuring they remained unnoticed. With a final glance at the swirling dancers, he gently took Elizabeth by the hand and led her out into the crisp night air.

"Driver!" James called out, his voice barely containing the anticipation coursing through him. "Take us to the Montague estate. And for God's sake, make haste."

As they climbed into the lavish carriage, Elizabeth's fingers brushed against his, sending shivers down his spine. The door slammed shut, sealing them off from the world outside, and they were alone.

"Finally," Elizabeth purred, her emerald eyes alight with mischief. "I've been waiting all evening for this moment."

James swallowed hard, unable to tear his gaze away from her full, inviting lips. He could feel the heat radiating from her body, and he longed to taste her forbidden fruit.

"Elizabeth," he groaned, the sound tangled in desire. "I must admit, you are an intriguing young woman."

"Intriguing?" She smirked, leaning in closer. Her perfume was intoxicating, a sultry blend of jasmine and amber that sent his mind reeling. "Not desirable? Not beautiful? Not wildly attractive?"

"You are quite desirable, Miss Elizabeth. Although I've only just met you, I am already captivated by your beauty," James confessed, his voice husky with longing. "And yes, I find you wildly attractive."

Elizabeth's laughter danced like music in the small carriage, filling the space with a melody of mischief and desire. Her hand trailed up James' thigh, inching closer to the core of his yearning. The tension between them crackled like electricity, igniting a fire that threatened to consume them both.

"Tell me, James," Elizabeth murmured, her voice laced with seduction. "What is it that you desire most?"

The question hung heavy in the air, mingling with the heat and anticipation. James could barely contain himself as his gaze locked onto Elizabeth's lips, imagining the taste of her sweet surrender.

"I desire to peel away the layers of propriety," he confessed, his voice low and urgent. "To explore every inch of your exquisite being."

A wicked smile curved on Elizabeth's lips as she closed the remaining distance between them, her lips brushing against James's with a tantalizing touch. The world outside the carriage ceased to exist as their bodies melded together, a symphony of desire and hunger.

Their kisses grew bolder and hungrier, each one stealing their breath away. Elizabeth's fingertips traced the contours of James's face, exploring every inch of his strong jawline and causing him to shudder with pleasure. Her tongue danced with his, igniting a fiery passion that threatened to consume them both.

Without breaking their heated embrace, James's hands wandered beneath Elizabeth's gown, his touch gentle yet possessive. He caressed her curves, mapping the terrain of her body with the reverence of an artist discovering a masterpiece. Elizabeth gasped against his lips, her breathing becoming ragged with need.

The carriage jolted as it hit a particularly rough patch on the cobblestone road, causing them to break apart for a brief moment. Their chests rose and fell in synchronization as they fought to catch their breaths.

Just as their mouths met in a searing kiss, Elizabeth took control, pushing him back against the plush velvet seat. Her hands roamed over his body with a hunger that mirrored his own, exploring every inch of him through the fine fabric of his suit.

"James," she murmured between kisses, "I want you to touch me."

Unable to resist any longer, James surrendered to Elizabeth's raw sensuality and allowed himself to be swept away in the carnal storm that raged between them.

"Tell me where you want my hands, Elizabeth," James whispered huskily, his breath hot against her ear. The tension in the carriage was palpable, and every nerve in his body thrummed with anticipation.

"Start here," she breathed, guiding his hand to her thigh, just below the hem of her dress. The contact was electric, sending a jolt of longing through them both as their eyes locked in mutual desire.

"Fuck, your skin is so soft," he groaned, his fingers slipping higher beneath the delicate fabric, inching their way towards the apex of her legs.

"Keep going," she urged, her voice laced with need. "Just a little more."

As his fingers reached their destination, he found her intimately wet and ready for him. Their gazes remained locked, and Elizabeth bit her lip, a flush spreading across her cheeks.

"Touch me there, James," she instructed, her voice quivering as she spread herself open for him.

"Like this?" he asked, stroking her exposed flesh with a gentle touch that elicited a shuddering moan from her lips.

"Harder," she demanded, her eyes glittering with challenge. "Make me feel it."

James obliged, increasing the pressure and speeding up his movements, the slick sounds filling the carriage. Elizabeth's breathing became ragged, her chest heaving as she struggled to hold back her climax.

"Take off your trousers," she panted, her own hand reaching for the bulge straining against the confines of his pants. "I want to see you."

He quickly shed his clothing, revealing his throbbing erection.

"Stroke yourself while you touch me," she commanded, her eyes never leaving his as he complied. The sight of him pleasuring himself was almost enough to send her over the edge.

"Fuck, Elizabeth," James grunted, his hand pumping in time with his fingers buried within her. "I'm so close."

"Me too," she gasped, pleasure building like a tidal wave inside her. "Don't stop."

Together, they brought each other to the brink, their climaxes crashing through them in a torrent of ecstasy. Panting and spent, they clung to one another in the aftermath, their bodies slick with sweat and satisfaction.

"James," Elizabeth murmured, her voice soft and sated, "That was... incredible."

"Agreed," he replied, his chest still heaving from the intensity of their shared experience. "Absolutely unforgettable."

3

As the carriage finally came to a halt in front of the grand Montague estate, Elizabeth panted heavily, her body still throbbing with pleasure from their intense dalliance. They quickly dressed and made an attempt to straighten up before the driver opened the carriage door.

Mr. Montague, clad in his night robe, stepped out from the shadows, his face a mix of surprise and annoyance at the sight of his daughter emerging from the carriage with a man whose clothes were disheveled and rumpled like hers. "Elizabeth, is everything alright?" he asked brusquely, his voice betraying his disapproval.

James quickly stepped forward, his own breathing ragged, "Yes, sir. Everything is fine. We had some trouble on our way back, that's all," he lied.

Mr. Montague narrowed his eyes, but didn't press further, instead thanking the coachman and dismissing him. As the driver climbed back up to his perch, James helped Elizabeth down from the carriage, his rough hands trailing down her back, causing shivers to run up and down her spine. She arched into him slightly, her body still craving more of his touch.

"Father," Elizabeth began, "might I know why I need a guard?" She knew what he was up to; she could see it in his eyes. He gave a sigh of resignation before replying about some shady business dealings he had made that required extra protection for his daughter – always so precious and fragile in his mind. Furrowing her brows, she conceded to having James around due to these "threats" just this once, knowing full well she wouldn't be able to escape him tonight anyway.

With that taken care of, they parted ways for the night. James would be staying on the estate down the hall from Elizabeth. They shared one last glance before going their separate ways, the lust still smoldering between them unspoken but palpable. Later that night, under the cover of darkness, Elizabeth heard a soft knock on her door. She knew who it was—their passion earlier hadn't gone unnoticed by either of them. She opened it slightly, revealing James standing there shirtless with an erection straining against his pants. Without a word, he pulled her into an intense kiss as he pushed his way inside.

"Elizabeth," he whispered, his voice rough with arousal, "Do you want me as much as I want you?"

She nodded, her lips slightly parted, her breasts rising and falling rapidly under her corset. "Yes," her voice faint and tremulous. She couldn't look at him directly, instead focusing on the wall behind him.

James stepped forward, his chest pressing against the door, trapping her between him and the wood surface. She felt the bulge in his pants against her stomach, and bit her lower lip, wondering if he would try something more. His hand slid up her arm, tracing the lace of her nightgown's sleeve before cupping her jaw gently, forcing her to look at him. His eyes held a mixture of lust and concern.

"I've never wanted anyone like I want you," he breathed.

Her heart raced in anticipation as he leaned in, his lips brushing against hers tentatively at first, coaxing them apart with his tongue. Their tongues danced, tasting each other. Elizabeth's whole body shook with excitement as he explored every corner of her mouth. Their rhythm increased, bodies molding together, igniting a hunger deep inside her that demanded to be sated. She moaned softly into his mouth, her hands fumbling with his cravat, needing more skin-on-skin contact. She pulled back, panting, her lips swollen from their kiss. "I need you," she confessed. "Please, take me now."

The air was thick with desire as they made their way to her bed. They didn't bother with preamble, tearing off each other's clothes in haste. Each touch sent shockwaves of pleasure through them. Elizabeth gasped as James's hands found her throbbing core, already drenched from their encounter in the carriage. He plunged two fingers inside her, his thumb circling her clit, and she screamed out his name. She arched her back, meeting his thrusts, begging for more. Her nipples were hard peaks against his chest as he sucked and licked them hungrily. She tasted herself on his lips, moaning as he continued to work her body into a frenzy.

She felt his hard cock pressed against her thigh and reached down and grabbed it with her hand. She stroked him slowly, her movements matching the rhythm of his fingers inside her. James groaned, his head falling back, overwhelmed by the pleasure coursing through his body. Elizabeth could feel him twitch in her hand, the need for release evident in the way he throbbed against her palm. With a teasing smile, she guided him to her entrance, and he entered her with a deep, forceful thrust.

The walls of her sex clenched around him. Her nails dug into his shoulders, leaving traces of red on his skin. Their hips slapped together in a frenzied rhythm, their breathing heavy and erratic. Desire burned through them both like wildfire. They moved together, lost in the heat of the moment. Every grunt and moan echoing through the empty halls. Elizabeth's body tightened, preparing to release.

"Let go, Elizabeth," James commanded, his voice rough and demanding. She screamed his name as they both climaxed, their bodies shuddering together. Sweat glistened on their skin, mingling as they caught their breaths. He collapsed beside her, pulling her close. She smiled softly against his chest, her cheek resting on his heartbeat as they both recovered. After what felt like an eternity, they finally managed to catch their breath and disentangle themselves from each other's clinging embrace. They got dressed quickly, but not before stealing one last lingering glance at each other before James went back to his room.

4

The morning sun filtered through the delicate lace curtains, casting a warm glow upon Elizabeth as she lay in her sumptuous four-poster bed. She could still feel the lingering touch of James's hands on her body from the previous night's passionate encounter. As she sipped her tea, her mind drifted back to their shared moments of ecstasy, each memory causing a shiver of desire to course through her.

"God, that man knows how to make a woman quiver," she thought to herself, her body tingling at the vivid recollection of their heated lovemaking.

The sudden sound of angry voices and the clamor of footsteps outside her bedroom window jolted Elizabeth from her reverie. Peering through the curtains, she saw a disheveled man waving his fists, shouting obscenities towards her father's estate, with a group of several other men also yelling. It didn't take her long to recognize the leader as one of her father's former business associates who had lost a fortune due to Mr. Montague's cunning tactics.

"Damn you, Montague!" the man bellowed, his voice hoarse with rage. "You'll pay for what you've done!"

Quickly, the guards stationed around the perimeter of the estate sprang into action, moving to subdue the irate intruder and his crew. The commotion grew louder, escalating into a cacophony of shouts and the clash of metal against metal.

Elizabeth felt a chill of fear, despite the warmth of the sun on her skin. Her heart raced, and she knew she needed protection from whatever danger might come her way. Just as panic began to set in, the door to her bedroom burst open, revealing James, his chest heaving and eyes filled with concern.

"Elizabeth, are you alright?" he asked urgently, his voice laced with both worry and determination.

"James! I'm fine, but there are men outside, threatening my father and our home," she replied, her voice trembling.

"You are safe," he commanded, his eyes never leaving hers. "I will protect you at all costs."

As he moved to close the door behind him, Elizabeth's thoughts raced. She knew James would do everything in his power to keep her safe, but she was afraid. The intensity of the situation only heightened her desire for him.

"James, we must hide!" Elizabeth whispered urgently as they heard the angry shouts from outside.

"Follow me, Elizabeth," James said quietly, taking her hand and leading her down a hidden passageway in the manor. The air was heavy with anticipation and uncertainty, but Elizabeth trusted James implicitly, knowing he would keep her safe from harm.

As they hurried through the dimly lit corridor, Elizabeth began to feel safe again. She noticed how James' muscles flexed beneath his shirt with every stride. Her body ached with desire for him, despite the danger they faced.

At last, they reached a small, secluded chamber deep within the manor. Once inside, James locked the door and surveyed their surroundings. The room was dimly lit by flickering candlelight, casting shadows that danced across the walls. A plush velvet chaise lounge sat against one wall, draped in silk sheets – an unexpected sanctuary amidst the chaos outside.

Elizabeth felt herself drawn to him, as if pulled by an invisible force. The intensity of the moment, coupled with their passion from the previous night, had ignited a fire within her that demanded to be stoked.

"Then let's not waste another moment," she murmured, reaching for him, her fingers trembling with desire.

"Elizabeth, you are simply irresistible," James growled as he captured her lips in a searing kiss. Their tongues tangled together, fueled by the raw urgency and desire pulsing between them. As their mouths explored each other, their hands roamed, seeking to satisfy the lust that had been ignited by their perilous situation.

"Touch me, James," Elizabeth gasped as he traced his fingers along the curve of her breasts, sending shivers of pleasure racing down her spine. "Make me forget everything but you."

"Your wish is my command," he replied, his voice thick with desire. He expertly unfastened her gown, letting it pool at her feet before lifting her onto the chaise lounge.

"Elizabeth, you're so fucking beautiful," he said, drinking in the sight of her naked body. His erection strained against his trousers, desperate for release.

"Then come here and take me," Elizabeth whispered, her eyes locked on his as she spread her legs wide, inviting him into her most intimate embrace.

Without another word, James shed his clothes and joined her on the chaise lounge, his hands finding her breasts, teasing and pinching her nipples until they were hard peaks. As he moved lower, his mouth found her core, tasting her wetness and eliciting moans of ecstasy from her parted lips.

"James, I need you inside me. Now!" Elizabeth pleaded, unable to bear the exquisite torture any longer.

"God, yes," he agreed, positioning himself at her entrance before thrusting deep inside her, filling her completely. The sensation was overwhelming, and they both cried out in unison, each lost in the primal rhythm of their bodies moving together.

"Fuck, Elizabeth, you feel incredible," James groaned as he drove into her again and again, his pace relentless.

"Harder, James!" Elizabeth urged him, her back arching off the chaise lounge as pleasure threatened to consume her.

"Like this?" he asked, slamming into her with a force that left them both breathless. Their moans and cries echoed through the hidden chamber, mingling with the sounds of their skin slapping together.

"James, I'm close," Elizabeth gasped, feeling the pressure building deep within her. Her body tensed as the first wave of orgasm washed over her, followed by another and another. With a final, desperate cry, she shattered apart in James' arms, clutching him tightly as ecstasy consumed them both.

"Elizabeth!" James cried out, his own release crashing down upon him like a tidal wave. He buried himself deep inside her, their bodies shuddering together as they rode out the last waves of pleasure.

Finally, spent and breathless, they collapsed against each other, limbs tangled and hearts racing. The world beyond their hidden chamber seemed to fade away, leaving only the echoes of their passion and a love that burned brighter than any danger they might face.

"Whatever happens next," James whispered softly against her ear, "know that I will always protect you."

"James," Elizabeth murmured, her eyes shining with love and devotion, "you are amazing."

5

The fading echoes of their breathless moans still hung in the air as James and Elizabeth reluctantly disentangled themselves from one another. The musky scent of their lovemaking clung to their heated skin, leaving a heady perfume that threatened to draw them back into the passionate embrace they had just shared. But time was of the essence, and they could not afford to surrender to their desires any longer.

"Damn, we need to get dressed," James muttered, his voice rough with lust as he surveyed their scattered clothing on the floor. He watched as Elizabeth bent down to retrieve her stockings, admiring the curve of her spine and the way her ample breasts swayed beneath her.

"James," she whispered, catching him staring. A wicked grin played on her lips, and she raised an eyebrow suggestively. "Eyes on the task at hand."

"Can't help it, love," he replied, flashing her a roguish smile before pulling on his trousers. "A man can't be blamed for being captivated by such beauty."

The sound of silk rustling filled the hidden chamber as they hurriedly dressed, each stolen glance between them crackling with electric tension. As Elizabeth pulled on her corset, she remembered the sensation of James's calloused hands gripping her bare waist, his mouth trailing hot kisses along her collarbone. She shivered despite herself, and James noticed.

"Are you cold, darling?" he asked, concern temporarily overpowering the ever-present hunger in his eyes.

"Quite the opposite," she answered with a teasing smile, buttoning up her dress. "But we must focus on the present, James. We have other matters to attend to now."

"Right," James sighed, fastening the last buckle on his boots. He moved towards the door of the hidden chamber, pressing his ear against it to listen for any signs that the attack was over. There was nothing but an eerie silence, causing James's heart to pound in his chest. Were they still in danger? Would they be discovered?

"Anything?" Elizabeth whispered, her eyes wide and filled with worry.

"Nothing," he murmured back, his hand tightening around the doorknob.

"Ready?" James asked, his voice a sultry whisper against Elizabeth's ear. Elizabeth nodded, her chest heaving slightly from the lingering excitement. James took her hand in his strong grip and together they stepped out of the hidden chamber, holding their breaths as they ventured into the unknown.

Their footsteps were light and cautious as they navigated the dimly lit corridors, the shadows dancing across their faces. The scent of burning wood hung heavy in the air, making their hearts race with anticipation. As they turned the corner, they were met with the sight of Mr. Montague, Elizabeth's father, standing tall and unharmed in the center of the grand foyer.

"Father!" Elizabeth gasped, releasing James's hand to rush towards him. He embraced her tightly, relief flooding his aged features.

"Thank heavens you're safe, my dear," he murmured into her hair, causing a pang of guilt to prickle within her. She glanced over her father's shoulder at James, who stood watching them with a smoldering intensity.

"James," Mr. Montague said, releasing Elizabeth and turning to face him, "I cannot thank you enough for protecting my daughter during this chaos." He extended his hand, which James shook firmly, doing his best to hide the knowing smirk that threatened to break free.

"Of course, sir," James replied solemnly, his eyes never leaving Elizabeth's. "It was my honor to keep her safe."

As the three of them discussed the events that had transpired, James let his thoughts drift back to the hidden chamber and the passionate encounter they had shared. The way Elizabeth's body had felt pressed against his own, the desperate sounds that had escaped her lips – it was enough to make his entire being ache with longing.

Elizabeth, too, seemed lost in thought, her cheeks flushed and her breathing shallow as she recalled the illicit affair they had just indulged in. She could feel the weight of James's gaze on her, and the knowledge that he alone knew of their secret rendezvous made her mind race with a mix of excitement and trepidation.

"Thank you again, James," Mr. Montague said, clapping him on the shoulder. "Your loyalty and bravery will not be forgotten."

James bowed his head, struggling to keep his voice steady as he replied, "I live to serve, sir." As he straightened, he locked eyes with Elizabeth once more, the intensity of their shared desire burning through the room like wildfire. They both knew that though danger had passed for now, the true challenge lay in keeping their passionate secret hidden from the world.

"Father?" Elizabeth called out.

"Yes, my dear?"

"I think I've changed my mind about having a full-time guard. I feel much safer with James around."

"Really? Well, that's good to hear. I have no plans to relieve him of his duties. You never know when we might have another dangerous situation on our hands."

"Thank you, Father," she said as she smiled coyly at James. "I'm glad to hear it."

THE END

ABOUT THE AUTHOR

Eliza Finch is a writer of short historical erotica. Check out some of her other work on Amazon and Kindle Unlimited.

All of Eliza's Books on Kindle Unlimited:
https://amazon.com/author/elizafinch

Sign up for Eliza's newsletter:
https://elizafinch.com

Get a FREE erotic short story by Eliza Finch, *Indebted to the Baron*:
https://BookHip.com/KBQKDNW